It's Always There

This book belongs to:

....

Text by Louise Shanagher
Design and illustration by Rose Finerty

It's Always There

First published 2014 by Book Hub Publishing
New edition 2018

THE LILLIPUT PRESS
62–63 Sitric Road, Arbour Hill
Dublin 7, Ireland
www.lilliputpress.ie

ISBN 978 1 84351 725 2

10 9 8 7 6 5 4 3 2

This is the first book in the Mindfully Me series.

Printed in Spain by Castuera

A Note for Parents and Teachers

Mindfulness is the practice of paying attention to the present moment on purpose and non-judgmentally. This book introduces 'mindfulness of the breath', or mindful breathing, to children. Mindfulness is a practical and effective self-care tool and has many wonderful benefits. Mindfulness can help children to relax, clear their minds and manage difficult situations, thoughts and feelings. Practising mindfulness helps children to connect with themselves, increasing confidence, self-awareness and well-being. Some of the best aspects of mindfulness are that it is free, can be done almost anywhere and, once learned, becomes a tool for life.

How to use this book

You can use this book to guide children through a simple meditation based on awareness of breath. To begin, ask the children to put their hands on their stomach and to feel it move in and out as they breathe. Another method is to invite children to put their fingers under their noses and focus on the feeling of cold air on their fingers as they breathe in and warm air as they breathe out. Children can also put small soft toys ('Breathing Buddies') on their tummies and watch them move up and down with their breathing. Ask children to focus on their breathing for about thirty seconds at first. You can increase the time with them as they practise.

The 'here and now'

Explain to the children that, when they do this, it brings them into the present moment: the 'here and now'. You can explain that the 'here and now' means paying attention to what is happening right now. It means not thinking about something that has happened already, or something that might happen in the future.

Mindful breathing

Explain to the children that their thoughts and feelings are just like clouds in the sky: they are always changing and moving, never staying the same. As the children concentrate on their breath, ask them to let the thoughts that come up just drift away like clouds and invite them to gently bring their focus back to their breathing. It is a good idea to remind them of this regularly throughout the meditation. Remind the children that, like the blue sky behind the clouds, their breath is always there. You can assure the children that, no matter what is happening in their lives and however they are feeling, they can always connect with their breath like this. Remember – it's always there.

How to use the workbook pages

You can use the workbook pages to reinforce the message of the story and help initiate conversations about thoughts, feelings and experiences with children. Try to create an accepting and non-judgmental atmosphere as you help the children with the workbook pages. Reassure the children that there are no right or wrong answers: all our thoughts and feelings are OK. By talking about them, we can get to know ourselves better. Children can write or draw their answers into a 'mindfulness diary' that can be used every day as a way for children to express their feelings.

Younger children may be more comfortable talking through their responses rather than writing or drawing them. The Mindfully Me series is aimed at children aged four and up, and additional ideas for activities for different age groups up to eight years old can be found at **www.loulourose.net**.

Tips for teachers

This book is aligned with the Irish primary schools' SPHE curriculum and the Aistear framework. This book links particularly well with the strand 'Myself' and the strand units 'Self Identity' and 'Growing and Changing'. For tips on how to use this book in the classroom, lesson plans and other resources, please visit **www.loulourose.net**.

In this book you will learn a magical secret.

This is the kind of magic that you can use almost any time and anywhere.

You can use it every day, every week or as much as you like.

The best thing about this magical secret is that, when you use it, it helps you feel calmer, more peaceful and happier inside.

Are you ready to find out what the secret is

I have a little secret
that I'd like to share,
it's a very special secret
for children everywhere.

Sometimes when it's cloudy,
when the sky is dark and grey,
I think the blue sky's gone forever
and the clouds are here to stay.

Sometimes when I'm sad or cross
and worries fill my mind,
I think that things will never change,
that life is so unkind.

Then I use my magic secret
and it works so well each time.
I put my hand onto my tummy
and everything is fine.

I feel my tummy moving
as I breathe nice and slow.
I know I'm in the here and now,
I let my worries go.

I listen to my breathing
and forget about the rest,
my mind has started clearing,
this secret is the best.

Then, as if by magic,
I feel good again,
my mind is slowly clearing
and the sun is shining in.

Now my mind is calm and clear,
it's like the bright blue sky.
My thoughts are just like clouds —
they're only passing by.

Now you know the secret
to a calm and happy mind.
Just listen to your breathing —
it's always there, you'll find.

It clears away your troubles
until you're calm inside.
It clears away the clouds
to show the bright blue sky.

All About Me

● ● ● ● ● ● ● ● ● ● ● ●

Finish the sentences! You can write or draw in your mindfulness diary or tell someone your answers.

I am ... years old.

My name is ...

I like ...

I dislike ...

I really love ...

I care about ...

I wish ...

I don't like it when ...

I'm happy when ...

when I grow up, I want to ...

Weather Inside

Sometimes we feel sunny and sometimes we feel cloudy and stormy. Circle the weather you feel inside today or draw your own. Remember, there is no wrong type of weather to feel inside.

'Here and now'

I know I'm in the 'here and now', I let my troubles go. Write, draw or tell someone what you see, smell, touch, hear and taste.

I see	I smell

I touch	I hear

I taste

Only Passing By

Remember, your thoughts are just like clouds: they are only passing by. Write, draw or tell someone about some of the thoughts or feelings you have had today.

Activity 1E

I Am Thankful For ...

When we are thankful, we feel happy about the good things in our lives. Stick a picture of something you are thankful for into the heart.